JESUS LOVES

Danny and Jesse

THIS I KNOW, FOR THE BIBLE TELLS ME SO.

Love, Mama
Easter 2024

ISBN: 978-1-7322418-4-8
Library of Congress Control Number: 2019914532

Published by Swing High, LLC. Wheaton, Illinois.
First Edition, 2020. Printed in China.

Scripture quotations marked (NLT) are taken from the Holy Bible, New Living Translation, copyright © 1996, 2004, 2015 by Tyndale House Foundation. Used by permission of Tyndale House Publishers, a Division of Tyndale House Ministries, Carol Stream, Illinois 60188. All rights reserved.

Discounts are available for quantity purchases, and for churches, schools, and associations. For ordering information, visit swinghighbooks.com

Illustrations by Natalie Merheb, nataliemerheb.com
Book Design by Clay Anderson, design.clayanderson.com

This I Know

by Clay Anderson

illustrated by Natalie Merheb

SWING HIGH!
CHILDREN'S BOOKS

swinghighbooks.com

"For ever since the world was created, people have seen the earth and sky. Through everything God made, they can clearly see his invisible qualities—his eternal power and divine nature."

Romans 1:20 (NLT)

IT'S TIME TO GET UP! Oh, the big day is here!
Are we ready to go? I've been waiting all year!
It's our day of adventure, our day of exploring,
Of running and hiking and swimming and soaring!

When I went to sleep, it was rainy and cold.
But the sun has come out, and the sky is like gold!
I jump out of bed, there is so much to do.
With every new day, God makes everything NEW.

Jesus loves me, this I know,
For the sunrise tells me so.

WAKE UP, LITTLE GIRL! You're so precious to me.
My sweet baby sister, how cute could you be?
I'd prayed and I'd asked God to give me a sister,
And you're so much more than I ever could wish for!

God loves His children, each daughter and son.
And He gives us new life, just like you, little one!
Today, I will show you the wonders outside,
How all of God's marvelous world is ALIVE!

Jesus loves me, this I know,
For our baby tells me so.

Mom is packing the van like a cozy cocoon!

And you know what that means? WE ARE LEAVING, AND SOON!

Like butterflies bursting to try out their wings,

We're ready to go and do all kinds of things!

It's such a big world full of so much to see,
I wish we could fly like the birds in the trees!
So what do you think we'll discover? Oh boy!
I love days like these that are full of God's JOY. 1 Peter 1:8

Jesus loves me, this I know,
For the butterflies tell me so.

WE'RE HERE AT THE BEACH! And my toes love the sand!
We splash in the waves as they crash onto land.
The seagulls are squawking, the air's full of smells,
I'm spying for dolphins and hunting for shells.

Just look at that water! So deep and so wide,
And brimming with life that is swimming inside!
My Dad says it makes him feel small like a child.
God's world is so big and so wondrous and WILD.

Psalm 104:24-25

Jesus loves me, this I know,
For the ocean tells me so.

WE'RE BACK ON THE ROAD, over slow rolling hills,

But our sweet little dog doesn't want to sit still!

With a wag of her tail, she is ready to run

In a wide open field, in the warmth of the sun.

Wherever I go, she is right by my side,
On bright happy mornings, or nights when I've cried.
She makes us all laugh, she is always so playful,
But what I love most is how God made her FAITHFUL.

Jesus loves me, this I know,
For our puppy tells me so.

A flash in the sky? Oh, please say it's not true.

It can't rain today. The sky has to stay blue!

But thunder rolls in with a rumble and BOOM!

If it doesn't stop raining, our day will be doomed!

But that's when Mom smiles, and reminds us to say,
"It's all in God's hands, so we wait and we pray."
A lightning bolt CRACKS! and my poor brothers cower.
Though storms can be scary, we trust in God's POWER.

Jesus loves me, this I know,
Even thunder tells me so.

Oh, can you believe it? The clouds have blown by,
And a rainbow is stretching across the blue sky!
When we don't expect it, GOD LOVES TO SURPRISE!
And sometimes the storms are His grace in disguise.

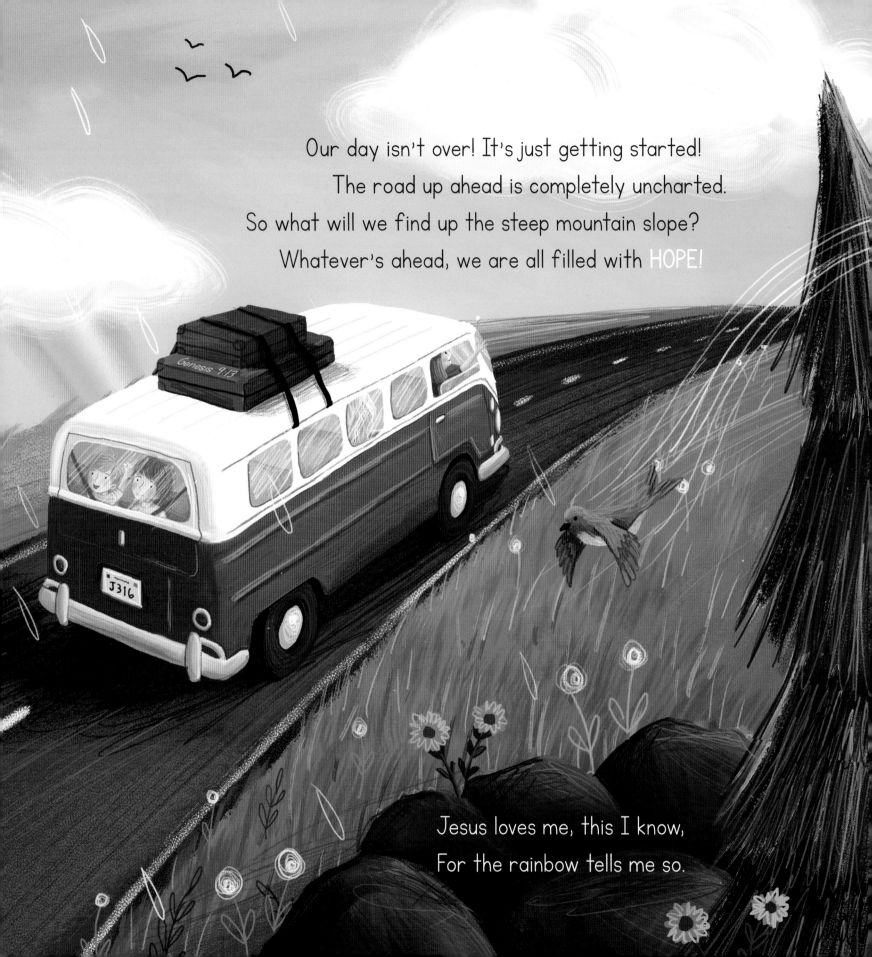

Our day isn't over! It's just getting started!
The road up ahead is completely uncharted.
So what will we find up the steep mountain slope?
Whatever's ahead, we are all filled with HOPE!

Jesus loves me, this I know,
For the rainbow tells me so.

We hop from the van, and start hiking a trail
Over brooks and on boulders, up hills and down vales.
And there at the top, as we round the last bend ...
"JUST LOOK AT THAT VIEW!" Like the world has no end!

God's world is so big, could He ever know *me*?
But He knows every sparrow, and every last bee.
And there in the rocks, He knows each flower blossom,
So fragile and frail, on a mountain so AWESOME.

Jesus loves me, this I know,
For the mountains tell me so.

Then just a bit further, right up at the peak,
I feel something gentle and cold on my cheek!
Floating down from the sky, landing right on my tongue,
LOOK! Each tiny flake is like no other one!

The snow gently falling is quiet and bright,
A magical wonderland sparkling in white.
God blankets the world in a loving embrace
With fresh fallen snow, like amazing new GRACE.

Jesus loves me, this I know,
For the snowflakes tell me so.

Back down the mountain, arrived at our camp,

Dad sets up the tent, and we all grab our lamps.

"MOM, DO YOU MIND IF WE GO ON A HIKE?"

And we're off to explore by the warm evening light.

Isaiah 40:8

Surrounded by piles of red, orange, and brown,
We kick them and crunch them and toss them around.
Though leaves are now falling, and done with their duty,
Each season of life is still filled with God's BEAUTY.

Jesus loves me, this I know,
For the fall leaves tell me so.

As the sun slowly sinks, a red glow in the sky,
A new light appears. It's as small as a fly!
A TWINKLE! A BLINK! As I reach out to snatch him,
He flits all about, till I finally catch him!

He crawls on my finger, so patient and slow,
And flashes his tail, like he's saying "hello!"
A bug that lights up? Oh, it just makes me ponder...
Is there no end to God's marvelous WONDER?

Jesus loves me, this I know,
For the fireflies tell me so.

Beneath a clear sky in a wide open field,
We sit in the grass, and we keep our eyes peeled,
And patiently wait until ... "LOOK! SHOOTING STAR!"
A streak through the sky! It's so near but so far.

The light of the stars, through the shadows of space,
Traveled millions of miles to brighten my face.
God is here and He's there and He's always wherever,
He's now and He's then and He will be FOREVER.

Psalm 19:1

Jesus loves me, this I know,
For the universe tells me so.

OH, WHAT A WONDERFUL DAY this has been!
We've had so much fun, I don't want it to end!
It's so full of memories we'll always keep.
But now it is late, so it's time for some sleep.

Snuggled tight in our tent, with a smile on my face,
My whole family is here, it's my happiest place.
The crickets are chirping, all others have ceased.
As their melody lulls me, I rest in God's PEACE.

Psalm 4.8

Jesus loves me, this I know,
For the crickets tell me so.

Jesus loves me, this I know,
For the Bible tells me so.
Little ones to Him belong.
We are weak, but He is strong.

Yes, Jesus loves me...
Yes, Jesus loves me...
Yes, Jesus loves me...
The Bible tells me so.

WITH OUR THANKS...

This book wouldn't exist without you!

Thank you for supporting the vision for this book, or encouraging our crazy dream, or a little bit of both.
Our prayer is that this book would glorify the God who called this incredible world into existence.

An extra measure of gratitude goes to...

Karen — you've put up with so many late nights as I've worked on this project. Love you so much. Thank you for pursuing this dream with me!
Dad — I love you, more than you'll ever know. And to Mom, who sang *Jesus Loves Me* to me almost every night — I miss you dearly.
The incredible community of children's authors from whom I have learned so much, and who have been so encouraging.

And to our backers on Kickstarter...

Andrew Fuller | Andrew & Kam Liu & Family | Dave & Cindy Heslinga | Dan & Clare Colwin & Family | Brian & Layne Ryks & Family
Clayton & Caitlin Edwards & Clark | John & Jen Berge & Family | Mark & Sharon Irvin | Ben & Stacey Kopchick & Family | The Neer Family
Aaron & Sheli Hayes & Family | Brian & Shelly Collins & Family | Jess, Amy, Alex & Emma Collins | Isaac Walton Getchell | Maureen Rader
Sarah Kate & Alice Eloise | Argyro | Virtuous Nyamesem Cornwall | Avelyn | Steven Czernek | Shiloh & Rebekah Dinkel | Shay & Landon
Breck & Remi | Felicity Tefft | Morenike Euba Oyenusi | Griffin & Greenleigh | The Thoreen Family | The Emery Family | Renee Mayse | Sophie
Heather Robyn | Hayden | Toby A. Williams | Mark Restaino | Samantha, Lillian & Alexandria | Soren & Fitz Perhach | Olivia, Adelyn & Gavin
...and so many more.

Finally, with gratitude to those of faith who have gone before us...

Anna Bartlett Warner, who wrote the words of *Jesus Loves Me* in 1860, and William Batchelder Bradbury, who added the melody in 1862.

FROM THE AUTHOR

For Avery, the one who first called me "Daddy."

When you were little, I would rock you to sleep with tears of joy in my eyes. You would look up at me and say, "I make you happy?" Yes. And you still do.

We waited so long for you, and you were an answer to so many prayers. When I held you that first time, I could say without a shadow of a doubt, "Jesus loves me, this I know."

And to all four of our precious kiddos: May you know how wide and long and high and deep is the love of Jesus for you.

FROM THE ILLUSTRATOR

For my twins, Ana and Estella, my double rainbow babies, and a promise fulfilled.

You were the answers to some very big prayers. Never have I felt just how much Jesus loves me as I did when I became your mom. In waiting for you, He prepared me for you. You may have arrived a couple months early, but with that, God was actually protecting you in countless ways. Jesus loves me, this I know, because when I look at you, my two little rainbows, with my heart full of a crazy big love, I see God's promises fulfilled and His unconditional, greater love for us.

May you come to know that the love of the Lord never stops, His mercies never end and His faithfulness is great.

HOW DO YOU SEE GOD IN THE WORLD HE MADE?